For my son, Thomas Ellinas — G.E.

For Caz Royds — J.R.

First published 2019 by Walker Books Ltd
87 Vauxhall Walk, London SE11 5HJ

2 4 6 8 10 9 7 5 3

Text © 2019 The Shakespeare Globe Trust
Illustrations © 2019 Jane Ray

The right of The Shakespeare Globe Trust and Jane Ray to be identified as
author and illustrator respectively of this work has been asserted by them in
accordance with the Copyright, Designs and Patents Act 1988

This book has been typeset in Filosofia

Printed in China

British Library Cataloguing in Publication Data:
a catalogue record for this book is available from the British Library

ISBN 978-1-4063-7685-2

www.walker.co.uk

WALKER BOOKS
AND SUBSIDIARIES
LONDON • BOSTON • SYDNEY • AUCKLAND

SHAKESPEARE'S GLOBE

WILLIAM SHAKESPEARE
The Tempest

Retold by Georghia Ellinas

Illustrated by Jane Ray

Can you do magic?
I am Ariel, a spirit of the air. I can fly, ride on
the curled clouds and burn bright as fire.
Magic is in every part of me.

My noble master, Prospero, is a clever magician.
This story is about how my master and I used magic
to do strange, frightening, yet brilliant things.

Prospero was the Duke of Milan. As he's a man, not a spirit like me, he had to read special books on how to make magic.

He spent so long in his library that he did not see that his jealous brother, Antonio, wanted to become the Duke. Alonso, the ambitious King of Naples, and his brother, Sebastian, plotted with Antonio to overthrow Prospero and his baby daughter, Miranda.

One dark and windy night, Antonio bundled them into a
leaky boat and cast them out on the waters to an unknown fate.

A kind friend had hidden food and water in the boat.

Prospero made sure he took all his books.

They were too important to leave behind.

The boat drifted onto the shores of this beautiful island, which is full of sounds and sweet delights. But the island hasn't always been this way. Before Prospero was washed ashore, an evil witch, Sycorax, and her monstrous son, Caliban, ruled it.

Life was hard for me then. Sycorax hated me and
imprisoned me in a hollow tree for twelve long years.
Thankfully, Prospero heard my desperate crying and
released me from my torment.

But my new freedom had a price.
In return, I had to use my magic
to help Prospero.

For many years I served my master faithfully. But Caliban thought
the island belonged to him. He hated us and wanted us to leave.
Prospero made him chop and carry wood as punishment.

I watched Miranda grow into a beautiful young woman.
She loved her father dearly, but she must
have been lonely sometimes.

One day, Prospero said that he had an important job for me.
His wicked brother, Antonio, was sailing past the island.
On board the ship were Alonso, the King of Naples, and his brother,
Sebastian. Alonso's son, Prince Ferdinand, who knew nothing
of his father's wrongdoing, was also with them.

This was Prospero's only chance to punish the men who
had stolen his dukedom. My master said that if I helped
him get his revenge, he would set me free.

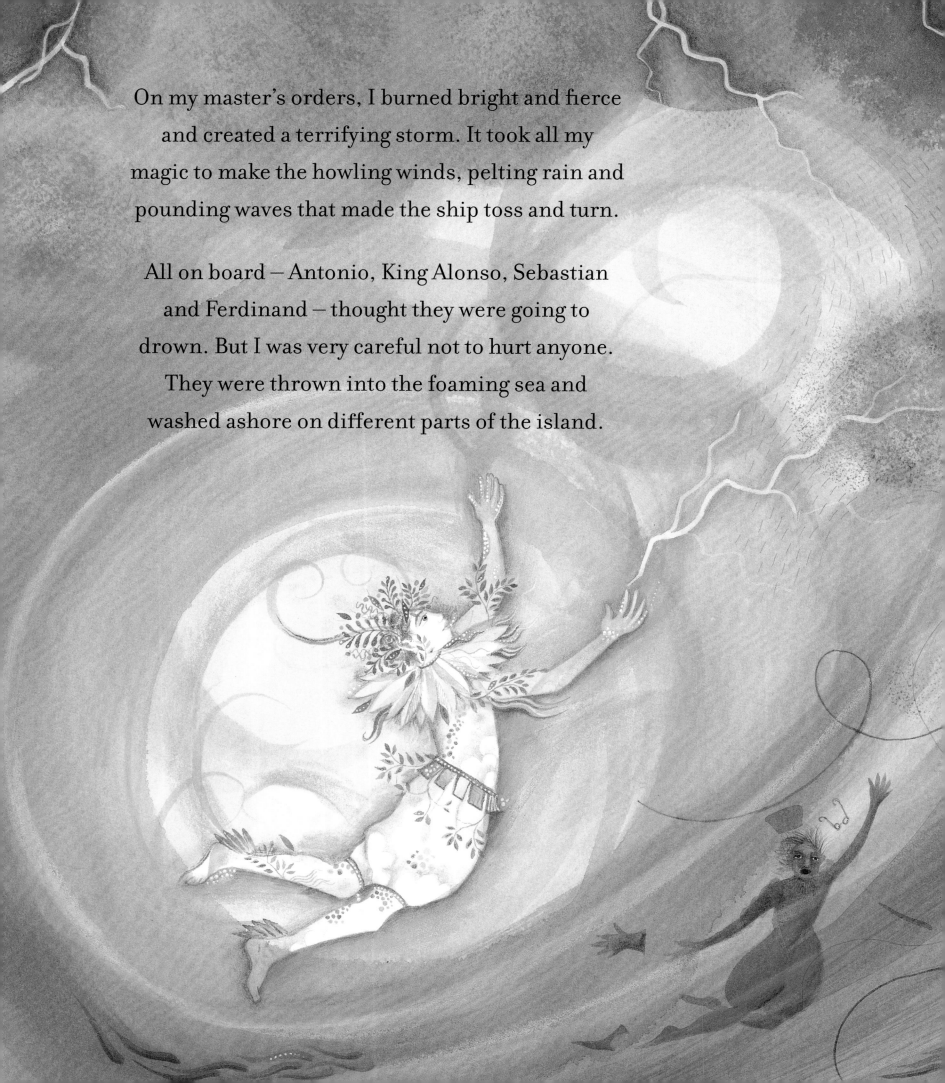

On my master's orders, I burned bright and fierce
and created a terrifying storm. It took all my
magic to make the howling winds, pelting rain and
pounding waves that made the ship toss and turn.

All on board – Antonio, King Alonso, Sebastian
and Ferdinand – thought they were going to
drown. But I was very careful not to hurt anyone.
They were thrown into the foaming sea and
washed ashore on different parts of the island.

Prospero wanted King Alonso to think that his son had drowned. I was sad to see Alonso crying for his lost son and Ferdinand crying for his lost father, but I had learned not to question my master. He had a very quick temper and didn't like it if I asked too many questions. I didn't want to go back into that hollow tree again!

Full fathom five thy father lies; Of his bones are coral made; Those are pearls that were his eyes: Nothing of him that doth fade

I cast a spell on Ferdinand and brought him to Prospero.
The best way to cast a spell is to sing it. My singing has calmed
the angriest animal. I sung to Ferdinand about his father.
This magic was easy after making the tempest.

But doth suffer a sea-change Into something rich and strange. Sea-nymphs hourly ring his knell
Hark! Now I hear them, Ding-dong, bell.

At my master's command, I broke the spell and Ferdinand opened his eyes. The first person he saw was gentle Miranda gazing at him in great surprise. Ferdinand thought she was a goddess.

In that moment, they fell in love.

Prospero was very pleased.

His plan was working.

I was so busy for the rest of that day doing
my master's bidding. I chased Caliban through the
forest because he had been up to no good — again.
I terrified my master's enemies, creating a feast
that vanished when anyone touched the food.
I even became a horrible creature and reminded
Antonio of the wrong he and King Alonso had done
to Prospero. I was here, there and everywhere.
But soon I would get my reward.

Prospero then commanded
that I bring Antonio, King
Alonso and Sebastian to his
cave. My master used his staff
to create a magic circle from
which they could not escape.

They could not move or speak,
but they could hear every word
he said. This was my master's
moment for revenge.

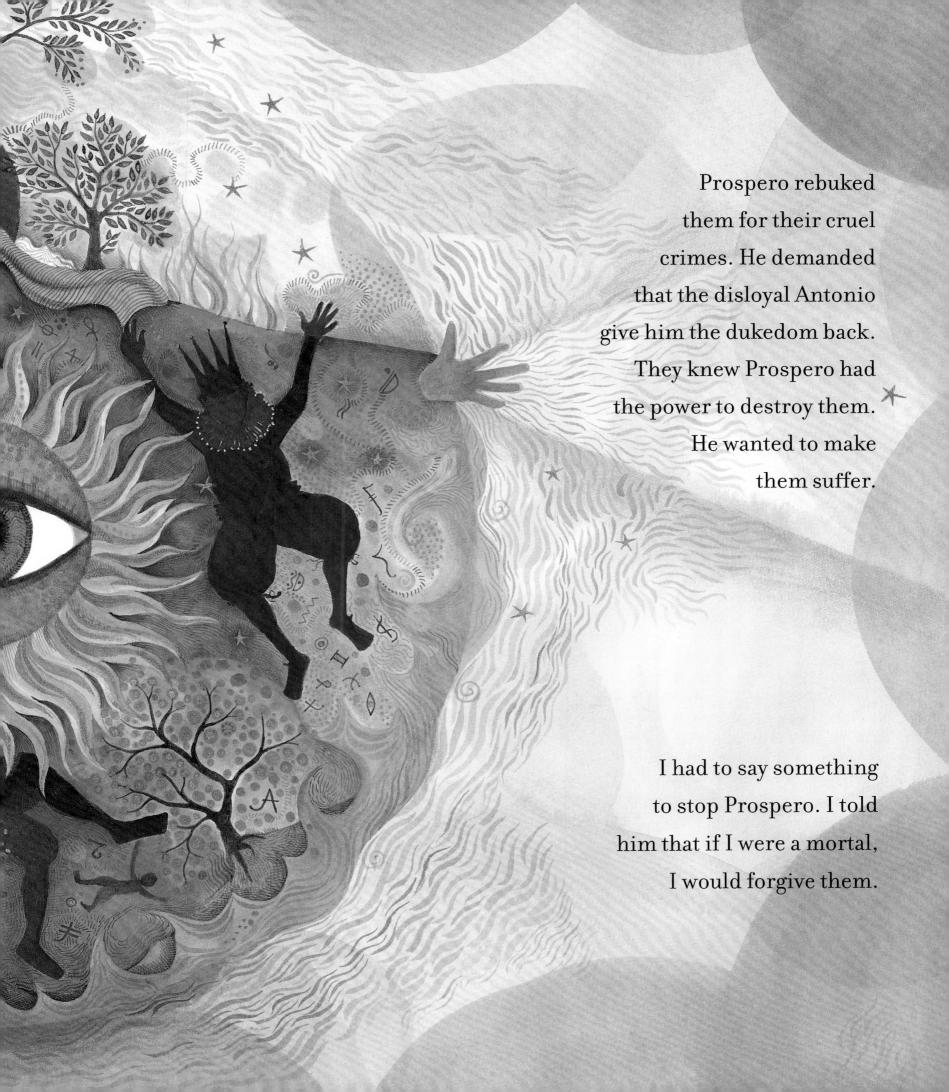

Prospero rebuked them for their cruel crimes. He demanded that the disloyal Antonio give him the dukedom back. They knew Prospero had the power to destroy them. He wanted to make them suffer.

I had to say something to stop Prospero. I told him that if I were a mortal, I would forgive them.

My master thought for a long time and, even though
it was very hard, he forgave them. He showed he had more
kindness in him than they had in them. He even forgave
Caliban and gave him back his island.

King Alonso was still sad because he believed his son was gone.
But Prospero then revealed Ferdinand playing chess
with Miranda. Alonso thought he was dreaming. He was
so happy. Miranda was to marry Ferdinand and
become Queen of Naples.

Prospero showed that forgiveness is greater than revenge. And from that day he gave up magic for ever. He broke his magic staff into pieces and drowned his books in the deep sea. Prospero could leave the island and return to his old home as the rightful Duke of Milan.

And then he set me free!

Where the bee sucks, there suck I:
In a cowslip's bell I lie;
There I couch when owls do cry.
On the bat's back I do fly
After summer merrily.
Merrily, merrily shall I live now
Under the blossom that hangs on the bough.

We are such stuff
As dreams are made on, and our little life
Is rounded with a sleep.
Prospero, Act 4, Scene 1